# Pleasant Fieldmouse's Valentine Trick

### By JAN WAHL

### Illustrated by ERIK BLEGVAD

Windmill Books and E. P. Dutton · New York

For his sister
LAURA JEAN

*Text copyright 1977 by Jan Wahl*
Illustrations copyright 1977 by Erik Blegvad
All rights reserved
Published by Windmill Books & E. P. Dutton
201 Park Avenue South, New York, New York 10003

Library of Congress Cataloging in Publication Data
Wahl, Jan.
Pleasant Fieldmouse's Valentine trick.
SUMMARY: Pleasant Fieldmouse devises a plan to bring
together his quarrelsome neighbors on St. Valentine's Day.
[1. St. Valentine's Day—Fiction.   2. Friendship—Fiction]
I. Blegvad, Erik.   II. Title.
PZ7.W1266Pm   [E]   77-3169
ISBN: 0525-61566-0
Published simultaneously in Canada by Clarke,
Irwin & Company, Limited Toronto and Vancouver
Designed by Ann Gold
Edited by Cary Rockwell
Printed in U.S.A.   First Edition

10 9 8 7 6 5 4 3 2 1

It had been a hard, wild, strong winter. Now it was Groundhog Day. Of course, everybody was eager to know whether the groundhog would see his shadow or not!

The forest creatures assembled outside of his house-hole located among the roots of an old hickory tree. They shivered in the sharp wind.

Icicles rattled on glazed branches above—plink! plonk! And the distant sun played hide-and-seek among gray clouds, while Sly Grasshopper went through the ground taking bets.

The best seats were on a tree stump where Pleasant Field-mouse and Mrs. Hedgehog, the champion worrier, sat.

"So come out, Snug Groundhog!" yelled Anxious Squirrel, rubbing his frosty paws and stamping his numb feet.

"Yes, step out and look for your shadow!" coaxed Cheerful Muskrat. "We want to get back home." They were bone-chilled and impatient. They wanted to learn if winter was over or not!

But Snug Groundhog stayed right where he was—in his warm, cozy bed under a ragwort blanket.

"Go away!" called Snug from the deep hole. "Look for your own shadow. It's a silly superstition, anyway!"

When all sensed they wouldn't learn that day whether spring
sunshine would begin and violets and cabbages would soon
grow—or if they'd have to suffer more cold and eat nettles and
thistles—they quarreled. The crowd started calling each other
names. Fistfights began. "Ouch!" "Quit it!"

Our Fieldmouse couldn't stand the bickering any longer. He shouted, "Listen! It's almost Valentine's Day. Won't that be fun?" He waited. Tongues stuck out.

*"BOO!"* *"PHOOEY!"*

The crowd hissed. Somebody hurled snowballs. *Wap!* Pleasant and Mrs. Hedgehog ducked.

Rushing home, Mrs. H. gasped: "I was afraid something awful would happen!" (She was wrong. It had happened.)

Her front window was broken. While she had been waiting for the groundhog to face his shadow, a thief had cleaned out her cupboard.

*No Cow Parsley Pie! No Slug Pudding! No Plum Bread or Bottled Parsnips—All stolen!*

"I'll starve!" she cried.

By following a trail of crumbs, Pleasant quickly found the two culprits sitting under a bush eating with stolen spoons.

Turnip jam was splattered over the villains, Terrible Owl and Tired Fox.

Mrs. Hedgehog raced into Pleasant's oak tree with him for safety. They bolted the door. Trying to calm her, the field-mouse brewed pinecone tea.

"I knew it!" she wailed. "That miserable fox!" She bawled into her shawl. *"I hate him!"*

Pleasant was sorry to hear this. He didn't want anyone to hate. Half the night he sat in a chair while the unhappy lady sobbed in his bed, "Blub, blub, blub!"

"I must go outside to think," he said.

The whole forest was in a sad, very ugly mood. *"What on earth can I do?"*

Through sparkling snow he marched, staring down at the ground.

"How can I cheer everybody up?"

Suddenly he hit upon a plan. He rolled it over in his mind and like a snowball it grew bigger and bigger.

Alas! Just then down swooped that monster, Terrible Owl, screeching horribly, "G-O-T Y-O-U!"

The owl grabbed Pleasant with steely claws, carrying him high into the air.

Our Fieldmouse was in a terrible state with apparently no way of escape. Then he remembered his plan.

"Um," said Pleasant to the owl with his teeth chattering, "Glad to see you—you are part of my plan, a very important part," he added.

"What?" asked the vain owl.

"Wouldn't it be more fun to play Cupid on St. Valentine's Day than to eat a mouse?" asked the fieldmouse.

"What?" asked the owl, again.

Pleasant whispered into his ear. Slowly the owl blinked his eyes, agreeing to meet the fieldmouse in the morning—or was he winking at his mischievous partner, Tired Fox, who was hiding behind a snowbank, as if to say—"I know what I'm doing?"

The fox slunk away, chuckling.

Soon it was to be Valentine's Day so a fine Valentine's Day sleigh was made out of scraps Pleasant found by the lake.

He enlisted the aid of Helpful Beaver and together the two decorated the sleigh with dried weeds, pressed flowers, feathers and ribbons.

Under Pleasant's direction, the birds agreed to make valentines out of birch bark and to search for tufts of fur or bits of cloth worn by each animal to give a personal touch.

Terrible Owl was dressed up in silverweed and matted leaves till he looked like Dan Cupid. Pleasant convinced White Tail Deer to pull the sleigh full of valentines from house to house on Valentine's Day.

Valentine's Day came with a bright and glittery morning. The sleigh stopped at every door. Pleasant hopped out, knocked cheerfully and handed everyone a valentine as well as a message written on a leaf. It said:

COME TONIGHT MISSUS
HETCHHOG'S HOWSE
BRING SOMTHING

If the householder thought of slamming the door or diving down a hole, he or she thought twice, for Dan Cupid (really Terrible Owl) fluttered in the air with a bow and arrow, hooting a *scary* tone!

And the owl's close pal, Tired Fox, rolled in the snow, howling with laughter.

Often-irritable Squire Beetle received a valentine from
Woolly Worm, who had a valentine from Squire Beetle.
Woolly had often tried taking Squire's nest in oak woodwork.
Now maybe they could share it!

The teacher—Miss Beaver—opened a valentine from Squeaker
Bat, who used to scare her. Squeaker's valentine was from Miss
Beaver—who used to chase him with a broom.

Lonely Widow Opossum got a valentine from lonely Old
Man Badger, who received a valentine from Widow Opossum!

Mrs. Hedgehog opened her valentine—it was from Tired Fox! Now she sat in her twig rocker, reading over and over a valentine from her enemy.

So it was Pleasant who gave a valentine to each in the name of the other. It was part of his plan.

St. Valentine's night seemed warmer. Stars hung above, decorating the sky, and a gold moon shone. The animals could feel green buds underground starting to sprout. Even Snug Groundhog decided to come to the party. Everybody agreed to bring something.

They walked in a parade, smiling, no longer grouchy. Some even sang or hummed.

They came to Mrs. H.'s house where the St. Valentine's sleigh was parked with presents piled high.

Mrs. Hedgehog peeked out from behind the curtains. Pleasant knocked on her door.

"Who is it?" she chirped, sticking her head out. She wasn't worried now.

Valentiners, holding little torches, snuggled together and chorused, "Happy Valentine's Day!"

"Oh!" she started to say, when at once Tired Fox, dressed as Cupid, sprang out from behind a shrub.

Snickering, he unhitched the deer and seized the reins.

Terrible Owl hooted in triumph, joining him, and both sped away with a gift-filled sleigh. One flying, one running!

Animals, birds and insects began to chase them. "I should have worried!" cried Mrs. Hedgehog. Frantic cries and sharp shouts rang out through the night.

It was hubbub and chaos! Mrs. Hedgehog was carried inside, put in her rocker and fanned.

Then down the lane were heard struggling shrieks—howls—
WHAM! It was awful!

*"Yow!"* *"Mercy!"*

Noises whizzed up the path, then silence. Suddenly a voice
resounded, deep as forest caves.

It was Grandpa Bear. With only his head poking through Mrs. Hedgehog's door, he said with a big yawn, "I was asleep in my log bed. The commotion woke me! I found this valentine beside me—

ROSES GROW RED,

VILETS GROW BLOO,

I GROW HUNGRY FOR SITE OF YOO.

"I don't know who sent it, but thanks!" growled Grandpa. "I also saw Sly Fox and Terrible Owl speeding by in a sleigh and guessed they must be up to something. They're outside now, along with all those presents."

Mrs. Hedgehog and Pleasant looked out. On top of the gifts sat the two guilty cupids, wrapped in vines. Mrs. H. hugged Grandpa's cold nose in delight. Imagine everyone's surprise when she announced:

"Let's still have the party! Tired Fox and Terrible Owl too! It's Valentine's Day!"

Her house was so tiny the guests spilled outside into the
shiny moon-glow and starlight.

Grandpa kept one eye on both owl and fox.

There were loud songs and jokes. Punch got squeezed from
berries.

Suddenly, a quick, hot breeze blew from the south. Spring shimmered in the air. "Our long hard winter is over!" All stood hushed.

The snow felt warm as white wool. It didn't really matter if Snug Groundhog had seen his shadow or not!

Those who had been angry drank punch and became chums. Mrs. Hedgehog forgave the fox because he sent her a valentine.

"Didn't know you *loved* me!" she yelled.

There still lay food left over for her cupboard. And she warbled, "La, la, la!"

Guests floated and drifted homeward, touching legs, wings, paws in new fellowship. Whistling, chattering. Why, you'd never guess only yesterday the forest wore a heavy heart.

As Snug Groundhog skipped back to his place, leaping and casting funny shadows below the full moon, Pleasant followed him.

"*Did* you or *didn't* you see your shadow on Groundhog Day?" he begged, scurrying close behind.

"I'll never tell!" giggled Snug, scooting into his deep, cozy hole. "NEVER!"

Nor did he.

The fieldmouse pondered:

"Just as well. We'll keep believing in his shadow's magic this way; it's good to believe in magic!" The fieldmouse trotted back to his oak tree, where he settled under moss blankets.

He felt drowsy and tired, but also quite content. His plan had worked. All the animals had come together for a time of good-heartedness and friendship. He even thought he heard Terrible Owl and Tired Fox serenading him, with Grandpa Bear joining in. But he wasn't sure. It was so warm he kicked off the covers.